TUMBLE TOWER

Anne Tyler

pictures by

Mitra Modarressi

ORCHARD BOOKS   NEW YORK

Orchard Books, 95 Madison Avenue, New York, NY 10016

E TYL

Manufactured in the United States of America. Printed by Barton Press, Inc.
Bound by Horowitz/Rae. Book design by Mina Greenstein.
The text of this book is set in 16 point Gamma Book. The illustrations are watercolor
reproduced in full color.   10   9   8   7   6   5   4   3   2   1

Library of Congress Cataloging-in-Publication Data
Tyler, Anne. Tumble Tower / Anne Tyler ; pictures by Mitra Modarressi.   p.   cm.
Summary: A very messy princess in a very tidy royal family has the opportunity to prove that
there are advantages to not being neat.
ISBN 0-531-05497-7.   ISBN 0-531-08647-X (lib. bdg.)
[1. Princesses—Fiction.   2. Cleanliness—Fiction.   3. Orderliness—Fiction.]
I. Modarressi, Mitra, ill.   II. Title.   PZ7.T937Tu   1993   [E]—dc20   92-44524

For Taghi Modarressi and Tezh Modarressi

Once upon a time, there was a very small princess who was known as Molly the Messy. She was the daughter of King Clement the Clean and Queen Nellie the Neat, and she had one little brother, Prince Thomas the Tidy.

Princess Molly and her family lived in a beautiful golden palace on an island in the middle of a lake.

Downstairs, the ballroom floor was polished as brightly as a brand-new shoe, and the dining room chandelier glittered like rock candy.

Upstairs, the master bedroom was so well organized that the King and Queen could find their royal robes every morning with their eyes shut.

Prince Thomas's room had shelves of toys arranged by size and color, and tin soldiers marched across his mantel in a perfectly straight parade.

But the tower belonged to Molly, and the tower was
a disaster.

When Molly took off her dress every night, she tossed it on
the floor. Some of her clothes had lain there so long that she
had outgrown them.

When she brought food to her room for a snack, she never, ever carried the dishes back to the kitchen. A seed from an old orange had sprouted into a tree beside her window.

And when she felt sleepy while she was reading a bedtime story, she just dropped her book among the blankets. Her bed was all lumpy and knobby with half-finished books.

King Clement said Molly's room was a disgrace to the
kingdom. Queen Nellie said she was ashamed to let people come
visit. Prince Thomas said, "Too bad she's not tidy and perfect,
like me."

But Molly said, "It's my own private room, and I like it just
the way it is."

She liked stirring her bare feet through soft clothes on a dark winter morning.

She liked finding a forgotten candy bar under a chair cushion when she was hungry.

She liked turning over in bed at night and knocking against her favorite book beneath the sheets.

Molly wasn't the only one who liked her room. The royal cat, Harriet, liked it so much that, when she had kittens, she stored them in Molly's closet among the heaps of fuzzy slippers.

And Molly's best friend, Princess Lila, liked it so much that every Saturday she begged to spend the night. She called Molly's room The Roomful of Riches.

King Clement called it a pigpen. He called it Sloppy City and
The Den of Disorder and Tumble Tower.

One cold November day, rain fell hour after hour and the lake began to rise. First it flooded the palace grounds and next it flooded the lower floor, and by evening, the stairs to the upper floor were halfway under water.

The King and Queen awoke in the middle of the night and discovered that the lake was lapping at the edge of their quilt. "Help!" they heard Prince Thomas cry.

So they waded across the hall to rescue him, and then they climbed to the tower. They knocked on Molly's door and called, "Molly? May we please, please stay with you?"

Molly opened her eyes. She said, "Well, of course," and she jumped out of her warm, dry bed and ran to let them in.

Prince Thomas was soaking wet, so she helped him into
some outgrown pajamas that were lying behind her toy chest.

King Clement was hungry, so she served him a half sandwich left over from her afternoon snack.

And Queen Nellie was thirsty, so Molly picked several oranges from the orange tree by her window and squeezed the juice into last week's cocoa mug.

Then the three of them climbed into bed with her, and to take their minds off their troubles, Molly read them a fairy tale that happened to be under her pillow.

When they got sleepy, she tucked them in tight, and Harriet and all six of her kittens nestled into the blankets around them to keep them snug.

In the morning, they awoke to find that the sun was shining and the flood was already shrinking. They breakfasted on doughnuts from Molly's sweater drawer, and by lunchtime they were able to go back downstairs.

Downstairs, the palace was so damp and muddy that the Queen almost cried.

But the four of them pitched in to clean up, and
by evening the rooms were neat again.

Every room except Molly's, that is.

To this very day, Molly's room is as messy as it ever was. Maybe it's even messier, because Ernestine, the royal dog, has recently decided to settle her new puppies under Molly's bed.

But the King and Queen and Prince Thomas don't complain about Molly's room anymore. In fact, they have even allowed their own rooms to get a tiny bit more cluttered.

This makes Molly feel right at home, whenever she drops by to kiss them good-night.